D0462977

PEANUTS®

Space Traveler
SALLY BROWN

by Charles M. Schulz
written by Ximena Hastings
illustrated by Scott Jeralds

Ready-to-Read

Simon Spotlight

New York   London   Toronto   Sydney   New Delhi

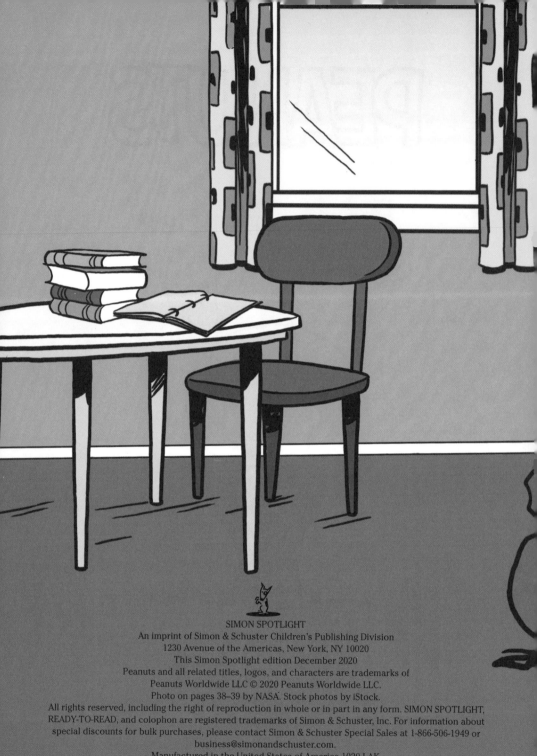

SIMON SPOTLIGHT
An imprint of Simon & Schuster Children's Publishing Division
1230 Avenue of the Americas, New York, NY 10020
This Simon Spotlight edition December 2020
Peanuts and all related titles, logos, and characters are trademarks of
Peanuts Worldwide LLC © 2020 Peanuts Worldwide LLC.
Photo on pages 38–39 by NASA. Stock photos by iStock.

Manufactured in the United States of America 1020 LAK
2 4 6 8 10 9 7 5 3 1
ISBN 978-1-5344-7972-2 (hc)
ISBN 978-1-5344-7971-5 (pbk)
ISBN 978-1-5344-7973-9 (eBook)

One day after school, Sally Brown turns on the television.

"Did you finish
your homework yet?"
Charlie Brown asks his sister.

"Not yet," says Sally.

Sally has to write a report
about a famous astronaut,
but she doesn't know
where to start.

"Go ask an expert,"
Charlie Brown suggests.

So Sally goes to visit
the World-Famous Astronaut:
Snoopy!

Snoopy puts on
his space gear.
Then he shows Sally
his special trophy.
"'First Beagle on the Moon,'"
Sally reads aloud.

*I'm the perfect subject
for your report!*
Snoopy thinks.

But Sally isn't so sure.
She goes to see another expert.

"What's your trouble?" Lucy asks.

"I don't know who to write about for my report!" wails Sally.

"Snap out of it!" Lucy says.
"You should write about Sally Ride,
of course!"

"Sally?" Sally asks.
"That's my name!"

"Sally Ride was
a very special astronaut,"
Lucy says.

"Follow me.
I'll take you to the *real* experts,
free of charge!"

Sally and Lucy arrive
at the library.
Peppermint Patty and Marcie
join them too.

The librarians help them
pull out every book
about space and astronauts.

"Wow," Sally whispers.
"Sally Ride was the first American
woman in space!"

"And she didn't just
go to space once," Lucy adds.
"She went twice!"

Sally Brown decides that
she wants to be
the next Sally in space.

"Astronaut training is hard work,"
Marcie says.
"That means we need
to start training now!"
Peppermint Patty replies.

Sally and her friends race over to Snoopy's doghouse.

The World-Famous Astronaut
knows exactly what to do.

First everyone does stretches
and jumping jacks.
Then Snoopy shows them how to
strap on their space gear.

Then he shows them how to
check the spaceship
for any problems.
"Everything looks good!"
Sally says. "All systems are go!"

With hard work
Sally, Lucy, Peppermint Patty,
and Marcie can become
the next women in space!

"What's going on out here?"
asks Charlie Brown.

"We are astronauts,
just like Sally Ride!"
Sally says.

"That's great!" Charlie Brown says.
"So, you finished your
homework?"

"I'll start it as soon as
I travel back from Mars!"
Sally replies.

"Oh, good grief!"
says Charlie Brown.

Read on
to learn more
facts about
women
in space!

Sally Ride

Sally Ride was born on May 26, 1951, in Encino, a neighborhood in Los Angeles, California. As a young girl, she was always interested in science and exploration. Her parents encouraged her to study hard and follow her interests.

In college Sally studied English and physics, which is a type of science focusing on the properties of matter and energy. She also liked playing tennis and running.

While Sally was a student, she found an ad in the school newspaper from NASA, the National Aeronautics and Space Administration. NASA was looking for women to join the astronaut program. Sally decided to apply, and she soon became one of the first six female astronauts at NASA!

On June 18, 1983, Sally became the first American woman in space. On her mission she was in charge of controlling a robotic arm that helped put communications satellites into space. On October 5, 1984, Sally returned to space a second time. This time she used the robotic arm to adjust antennas.

Sally left NASA in 1987. She went on to teach physics, encourage students to study science, and wrote several children's books about science.

Mae Jemison

Mae Jemison was born on October 17, 1956, in
Decatur, Alabama, and moved to Chicago when
she was three years old. She loved science,
dancing, and theater. When she got
to college Mae studied chemical
engineering and African and
Afro-American studies.

After becoming a
medical doctor, Mae
volunteered in the Peace
Corps as a medical officer.
Then she remembered her
childhood dream of being
an astronaut.

Mae was inspired by Sally Ride and applied to NASA's astronaut program. In 1987 she became one of fifteen people selected for the program.

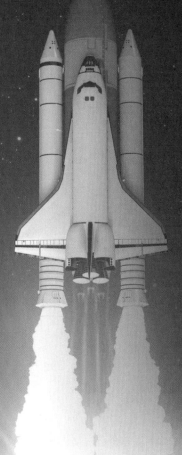

Mae became the first African American woman in space on September 12, 1992. She was a science mission specialist and conducted experiments to see how astronauts' bodies reacted to being in space for several days.

After leaving NASA, Mae went on to teach, start her own company, and lead the 100-Year Starship project that wants humans to be able to travel beyond our solar system within the next hundred years.

Do you know what a **spacewalk** is?
A spacewalk occurs anytime an astronaut in
space goes outside a spacecraft. Astronauts
go on spacewalks to perform experiments, test
equipment, repair spacecraft, and learn more
about space!

On October 18, 2019, NASA astronauts Christina Koch and Jessica Meir made the first all-female spacewalk. That means they were the first two women to do a spacewalk together.

The two women worked together for more than seven hours to repair a power controller on the International Space Station.

During an interview Jessica gave credit to the female scientists, explorers, engineers, and astronauts that helped pave the road for Christina and her. "We are following in their footsteps," she said.

Shoot for the stars!